Watch out!
I am HOOT OWL.
I am hungry.

And here I come!

HOOT OWL, MAS

Sean Taylor

Jean Jullien

To James – for taking Hoot Owl
under his wing! ~ST

I dedicate this book to Sarah, who
is as cute as Hoot; to my papa and
my maman, who read me stories that
inspired me; and to Mélane and Nico,
who grew up to them with me ~JJ

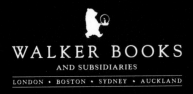

WALKER BOOKS
AND SUBSIDIARIES

LONDON • BOSTON • SYDNEY • AUCKLAND

First published 2015 by Walker Books Ltd, 87 Vauxhall Walk, London SE11 5HJ ✲ Text © 2014 Sean Taylor Illustrations © 2014 Jean Jullien ✲ The right of Sean Taylor and Jean Jullien to be identified as author and illustrator respectively of this work has been asserted by them in accordance with the Copyright, Designs and Patents Act 1988 ✲ This book has been typeset in Futura ✲ Printed in China ✲ All rights reserved. No part of this book may be reproduced, transmitted or stored in an information retrieval system in any form or by any means, graphic, electronic or mechanical, including photocopying, taping and recording, without prior written permission from the publisher ✲ British Library Cataloguing in Publication Data: a catalogue record for this book is available from the British Library ✲ ISBN 978-1-4063-4841-5 ✲ 10 9 8 7 6 5 4 3 2 ✲
www.walker.co.uk

TER OF DISGUISE

The darkness of midnight
is all around me.
But I fly through it as quick
as a shooting star.

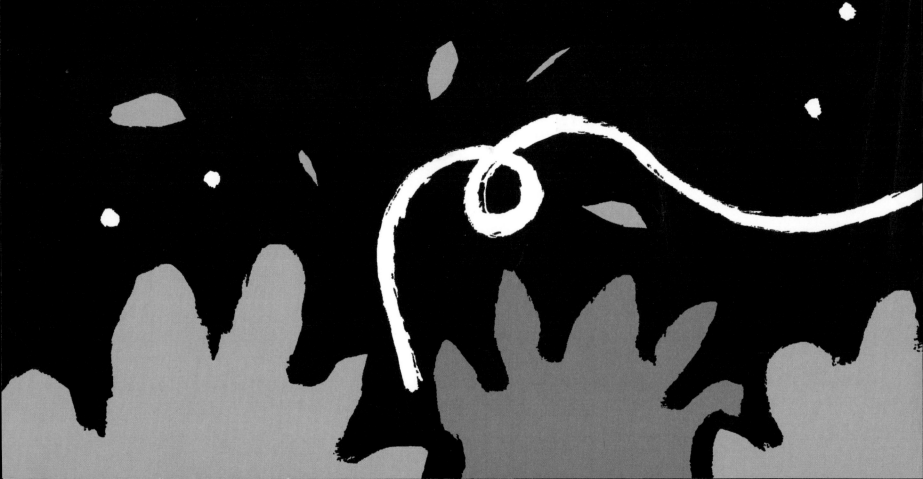

a tasty rabbit for me to eat!
Soon my sharp beak will be
gobbling the rabbit up.

Everyone knows
owls are wise.
But as well as
being wise,
I am a master
of disguise.

I organize a costume.

Look...

I disguise myself as ...

a delicious carrot.

And here I come!

The night has
a thousand eyes,
and two of them
are mine.
I swoop through
the bleak blackness,
like a wolf in the air.

And look there ...

a juicy little lamb stands
helpless in the cool of the night!

The lamb is a cuddly thing,
but soon I will be eating it.

Everyone knows owls are wise.
But as well as being wise,

I am a master of disguise.
I organize a costume.

Look...

I disguise myself as ...

a soft and fluffy mother sheep.

It is the perfect way to catch a lamb.

I wait.

It doesn't work.
But still...

I am HOOT OWL.
I am hungry.

And here I come!

The terrible silence of the
night spreads everywhere.
But I cut through it like a knife.

And look there ...

a delicious pigeon
stands trembling
in case a dangerous
creature-of-the-dark
(such as an owl)
may be passing by!

In a matter of moments
the pigeon will be
in my tummy.

Everyone knows
owls are wise.
But as well as
being wise,
I am a master
of disguise.

I organize a costume.

Look...

I disguise myself as ...

an ornamental
bird bath.

It is the perfect way to catch a pigeon.

I wait.

It doesn't work. But never mind!

I am HOOT OWL.
I am very, very hungry.

The shadowy night stretches away
forever, as black as burnt toast.

And look there ...

a mouth-watering pizza!

My eyes glitter like sardines
because I am sure the pizza will be mine.

Everyone knows owls are wise.
But as well as being wise,

I am a master
of disguise.

a waiter in a pizza restaurant.

It is the perfect way
to catch a pizza.

I wait.

They don't call me
Master of Disguise
for nothing.

I eat the pizza with my
deadly-dangerous
beak.

It is Italian-sausage flavour.

The last bite is as good as the first.

Then, tired but satisfied,
I transform myself
back into plain HOOT OWL.

I disappear into the dark
enormousness of the night.

I am gone.

And the
world
can sleep
again.

Until
HOOT
OWL
returns.